LUCY LUSCIOUS

For Your Eyes Only

This book was professionally typeset on Reedsy.
Find out more at reedsy.com

Contents

One

Bad Decisions

"Fuck this week!" I screamed, violently shoving the papers on my desk causing them to coalesce into a jumbled pile against the wall. I had had enough, hitting the stress level breaking point where all you want to do is curl up in the fetal position and cry like a little girl.

I wasn't going to cry though. My plan was much more eloquent—simply drink my problems away. There is nothing like copious amounts of alcohol to solve all life's problems.

I could really use a could lay too, like in a bad way. My battery-operated boyfriend was just not getting the job done lately. *Maybe I'll go out and find someone to take care of business for me.* I smirked to myself. *Hurray for bad decisions!*

One very hot, cathartic shower later and I was feeling marginally better. I definitely looked better. Especially now that I wasn't screaming at my paperwork anymore. I stood in front of my full-length mirror in just my black lace lingerie—essential for a night of drinking and bad decisions—trying to decide what to wear.

Do I go for sexy and sizzling hot, or cute and innocent sex kitten? I turned my back on my reflection to peruse the assortment of clothes scattered across my bed. *Definitely his place,* I decided as my gaze drifted over the rest of the disaster that was my room.

Ok, focus. Need clothes. I pulled a pair of bootcut jeans out of the pile on my bed. I know skinny jeans are all the rage these days, but I'm just not on board. They make me look like an upside down fruit. *Next I need the most cleavage-y shirt I can find.* Ten minutes and several outfit changes later, I had arrived at one killer look. Boot cut jeans, ridiculous heels and a corset style top that looked like it was laced all the way up the back but was really just a clever ruse. There were hook and eye fasteners underneath the fake lacing. This made it actually possible to put it on by myself.

***

The bar I frequented was hopping as always, full of twentysomethings on a mission. Most of them were probably on the same mission as me.

Okay, I thought, *step one, down as much alcohol as possible in as short a time span as possible.* I stepped up to the bar and one of the waitresses was on me like white on rice.

"Usual?" she shouted over the din.

"Yeah, and a Jagerbomb!" I yelled back, leaning over the bar to make sure she heard me. While she turned her back to pour my drinks I checked out the talent. I gotta say, one of the benefits of coming to the same bar every weekend was that ordering a drink became as easy as simply nodding in the direction of a waitress. Or holding up a couple fingers if I happen to be out with friends.

Tonight, I was alone though, my friends all occupied with other things and I wasn't very good company anyways. This week of overwhelming stress had made me bitter and angry.

Oh well, bombs away! A Jagerbomb appeared in front of me, and I pressed my cash into the bartender's hand. I downed the drink in a couple of swallows and slammed the neat little shot-glass-in-a-cup back onto the bar.

When I turned around, he was standing there. *Well hello.* I opened my mouth to say something hopefully more composed than that, but he beat me to it.

"Rough week?" he asked.

"Like you wouldn't even believe," I replied, "how could you tell?"

"There's nothing like a Jagerbomb to help you forget your problems." He smiled and leaned past me to signal the bartender, brushing his chest along my arm in the process.

I smiled back, tingling all over. Whether from his touch or the booze I couldn't tell, but there was definitely potential here.

***

His hand was up the back of my shirt. People were staring, but three shots and countless rum and cokes meant that I just didn't care. The music was so loud I couldn't hear myself think, and I desperately needed a cigarette.

I put my hand on the back of his neck. He misinterpreted my intention and pressed his mouth to mine. He tasted like whiskey and smoke and the promise something more. We kissed until I couldn't breathe, and I pulled back to gasp for oxygen.More people were staring. The second time I pulled him close I veered to the left and yelled in his ear.

"I need a smoke!" I jerked my head towards the door. We half walked, half stumbled out onto the patio, his hand was still up the back of my shirt. Vaguely it occurred to me that having his hand up there was destroying the illusion of my cool faux-corset top. However, if the night went where it seemed to be heading, that illusion would be shattered soon enough anyway.

We managed to snag a couple of chairs outside and I sat down maybe a little harder than was strictly necessary. I rummaged through my purse for a lighter until my handsome new friend produced one and held the flame in front of me.

"Thank you, kind sir," I said with a coy smile. "Sweet ambrosia." I sighed, exhaling that first heavenly drag.

He leaned in close to my cheek and whispered seductively,

"I know a few other tricks that you'll want to thank me for. Want to get out of here?"

"Hell yes," I replied, and tossed the end of my smoke into a nearby ashtray. We headed out the patio boardwalk to hail a cab.

"Are you cool coming back to my place?" he asked, his hand tucked into my back pocket. He gave my ass a gentle squeeze.

"Sure," I replied, "what's the address?" I handed him my phone to type it into an already open conversation. "Safety first." I winked at him.

He handed my phone back with a smile and nod as we reached the waiting taxis lined up on the curb and gave the same address to the driver. We climbed into the back seat and I finished off the text to my friend, letting her know where I was headed, and tucked my phone neatly into my bag.

"Now, what was that about your other tricks?" I asked as the cab pulled smoothly away from the curb.

"Oh, looking for a preview?" he asked smirking.

"Just making sure you're worth my time," I replied with a

smirk of my own as I ran my hand slowly up his inner thigh. I grinned as he shivered, and his eyes fluttered closed. "I could give you a pretty great preview of my own, no sense wasting time."

The hand travelling up his thigh slid up and around his lower back, leaning forward to press my body against his. My other hand gripped the back of his neck, pulling him in for another searing kiss.

He came to himself as our lips crashed together and shifted against me. He pressed my shoulders back hard against the seat of the cab and hiked one of my legs up to his hips. The other hand he wound through my hair, gripping hard. I moaned into his mouth at the rough pulling sensation.

He pulled his mouth back enough to take a breath and whispered against mine, "Hair pulling is yes then?" he asked with a tug.

"Oh yes," I moaned in reply and pressed my mouth back against his, tugging his locks in reply. He growled into my mouth with an answering yank and pushed his other hand up under my shirt. Finding himself unimpeded by a bra—no need for one with a top like this—he immediately went to work on my breast. He pinched and rolled my nipple between his thumb and forefinger, my hips lifting off the seat of the cab in an attempt to grind myself against him.

"Eager?" he asked, that smirk of his firmly in place once again. His talented hands still exerted just enough pressure on my scalp and at the same time playing my breast like an instrument built for him and him alone.

I reached between us and gripped his hard length through his pants. "I'm sure I'm not the only eager one."

Our driver interrupted at that moment with an abrupt, "We're here."

I blushed and fixed my shirt as my companion grinned at me and released my hair and breast to fish out his wallet. He handed the driver the fare plus a sizeable tip, which I appreciated, both as a former customer service employee and as a woman who was very aware that he had just sat through us blatantly fondling each other in his backseat without so much as a word of complaint.

With an embarrassed smile, I stepped out of the taxi and gently closed the door behind me. I shook my shoulders back, dismissing my momentary abashed feelings. Some dudes might find the shy, virginal look appealing, but I wasn't about to misrepresent myself. I was the sheer opposite of a blushing virgin.

My partner for the evening came to my side, and wrapped his strong arm around my waist. "My name is Kevin by the way," he growled into my ear. The arousal in his voice came through loud and clear.

I leaned back and trailed my tongue up his neck. "Lucy," I whispered with a light flick along the shell of his ear.

"Hot," he replied. Whether in response to my name or my tongue play I wasn't sure.

I let him lead me up the steps to his apartment building. We disentangled for a moment so he could negotiate the secured entry, then headed up a flight of stairs to arrive at his door. He grinned at me as he unlocked the door, and I was struck for a moment by his boyish adorableness.

He took my hand and pushed the door open, revealing a small and neat apartment. It was clearly a man's home, but not a stereotypical bachelor pad. As soon as the door closed behind us, he pressed me back against it, crashing his lips against mine.

He locked the door with a click, but it was a distant sound over the pounding of my blood echoing in my ears. I slid my hands up under his shirt and tangled my tongue with his. Reluctant as I was to pull away, we both needed air, and I needed to get this shirt off him so I could run my hands over his sculpted torso.

We broke apart, gasping for breath and I pulled his shirt violently over his head, tossing it into the living room. He took advantage of the momentary break to tug my hand and pull me towards what I assumed was the bedroom.

My heels clattered on the tile floor of the hallway and halfway there I pulled back on his arm, hard. His body collided with mine as I backed into the wall, reaching up to his neck to bring his mouth back to mine. My other hand explored that torso I had gotten just a taste of.

As we finished another breathtaking kiss, he tore his mouth away from mine and licked and sucked a trail up to my ear whispering, "I promise my bed is more comfortable than the wall." I smirked and allowed him to lead me the rest of the way down the hall to his room.

He was right in his assessment of his bed's comfort. I fell back onto the soft duvet, having lost my shirt somewhere along the way, and groaned aloud at the softness against my back. I stretched my arms above my head and arched my back, giving him a great view of my breasts.

His big hands ran roughly down my sides, dipping with the contours of my waist and hips. When he reached the waistband of my jeans, I heard that delicious growl again. He quickly unbuttoned and unzipped them, then knelt between my feet to yank them off my hips. I lifted my ass off the bed to facilitate the process, and once he got them to my knees he slowed down.

"Will these come off over your shoes?" he asked, eyeing my

heels with passionate hunger.

"Yeah," I replied, breathless. My own hands had wandered back down while he was dealing with my pants and were now circling my nipples in a slow tease. He grabbed the hems of my jeans and eased them over my heels. *Hurray for bootcuts! I thought. Who needs skinny jeans?*

Once I was successfully divested of my pants, Kevin kissed his way back up my legs. I moaned and twisted my hips, desperate for friction and a cock. When he reached the apex of my thighs, he slid my panties down the same path my pants had taken.

As I lifted my hips I moaned, "Let's fuck. Now."

"I knew you were eager." He chuckled as he tossed my panties to the side and grabbed my hips in his strong grip. He yanked me to the edge of the bed and lined himself up with my entrance. "Are you sure you don't want to…" he began, and I released one of my nipples to grab his tight ass and pull him towards me.

"I want your cock inside me," I ground out, "Condom first though," I remembered through my lust filled haze.

"Right," he replied, "Good call."

He released my hips, and I whimpered at the lack of contact as he fumbled through the drawer next to his bed. There was a tear and a hiss as he rolled it on, but I wasn't watching. The hand I had used to pull him to me had found its way to my clit and was going to town.

"Hey, hey," he said, turning back to me. "Don't get there without me."

"I would never," I breathed as he leant down and captured my mouth in another bruising kiss, one hand palming the breast I had been neglecting as he lined himself up with my sopping opening.

"Ready?" he asked.

"Oh yes!" I replied, and as he entered me, I gripped his hip, pulling him in deep right off the bat. "Omigod, yes, just like that."

"Like it deep huh? And hard?" he asked as he pumped in and out of me. Having lost the ability to answer coherently, I just nodded my head.

My hips lifted in time with his thrusts, seemingly of their own accord. We found our rhythm quickly, with him leaning down to kiss my neck and gently bite my earlobe. With each nibble I moaned and raked my nails down his back. He arched into each scratch and growled in response.

I ran my hands up and down his beautiful body and when his thrusting became more erratic I gripped his hips, urging him in deeper. I pressed my pelvis up hard against his, trying to get the friction I needed for release. He seemed to sense my urgency, and grabbed one of my hands from his side, guiding it between us so I could reach my clit, a gesture I greatly appreciated. I furiously rubbed my hard bundle of nerves, still thrusting in time with his as best I could.

Within moments I was screaming, head thrown back in ecstasy, my hips aimed to the ceiling completely out of my control. He followed me over the edge, thrusting his exquisite cock as deep as it would go as he spilled himself with a shout.

He collapsed on top of me, panting, and after a moment pulled out and rolled to the side. I laid there beside him, chest heaving as I came down from the amazing heights he had brought me to.

After a few minutes, we crept into awkward, post one-night stand territory when he turned to me and said, "Hi Lucy, I'm Kevin." He held out his hand over my bare chest as if to shake mine.

I laughed out loud, and reached for his hand, giving it a vigorous shake.

"Hi Kevin," I said, still breathless, "nice to meet you."

END

Two

Getting Wet

Warm water streamed down my back and toned abs as I pulled myself up on the edge of the pool. I pivoted my hips at the right height to set my bikini clad bottom onto the concrete edge. I pushed my long, dark hair back and sluiced the water out of it as best I could, causing a puddle to form around me. It was always nice to come in to work early enough for a couple of laps before I got up on the big chair to attend to my lifeguarding duties.

When I'd started lifeguarding as a teen it wasn't something I had meant to keep doing long term. For most people it was a high school job, a way to pass the summers and make some cash without having to endure the abuse of being a cashier or fast food employee. I hadn't anticipated that I would fall in love with job, that I would transition from just part time guarding to swimming lessons, that I would treasure watching each new kid earn their flippers and learn to swim. But I had, and now here I was at 25, working at the pool full time and loving every second of it.

One of the more positive aspects of the job was the fact that I got to spend so much time in my bathing suit. Clothes are such a pain in the ass, and work uniforms even more so. I loved coming to work everyday and throwing on my suit and sitting out in the sun during the summer or inside the heated indoor pool building in the winter.

However, I had recently encountered a problem that was interfering with my ability to enjoy my job. Or rather it was enhancing it, but possibly a little bit too much. My old boss had retired, and I had gotten promoted to co manager. The "co" was this important part because I wasn't just put right in charge, which was fine with me—I didn't want to do all that paperwork alone anyways. The problem was the man the town council had hired in to be the other manager, Billy. There was nothing wrong with him, oh no, there was everything right with him.

He was my age and in impossibly good shape, likely due to all the swimming. He had a photo-ready smile and was so easy to get along with it was almost criminal. Several intricate tattoos danced their way down his arms, and he had the uncanny ability to have perfect hair before and after he'd been in the water. I found myself sometimes looking for things that could possibly be wrong with him. Any chink in the perfection façade, but I found nothing. And the more time I spent obsessing about his perfection the more my crush on him intensified.

It didn't help that he was a shameless flirt. I wasn't sure if that was just his personality or if it indicated something more. I hadn't known him long along enough to know. Deep, dark, lust-filled parts of me hoped it was something more. Hoped he was flirting with me because his thoughts were as consumed with perverse desire as mine were.

He'd saunter by me on the deck with his swim trunks sitting sinfully low on his hips, and then wink mischievously. Or he'd lean over me while I was sitting in the office chair doing paperwork, always to help or give his opinion, but also pressing his washboard abs against my bare shoulder. When we talked, he smiled and laughed in all the right places. He didn't stare but I would notice his eyes wandering over the curves of my bathing suit. Or lingering on my tanned thighs when I walked by.

On this particular day, my feet still dangled at the waters edge, my hair dripping down my back as the sun warmed my skin. Billy came out of the pool house and headed towards me. I tipped my head back to watch him, tanned skin burnished by the sun, his bright blue eyes shielded by sunglasses.

"Have a good swim, Elle?" he called as he approached, and I was forced to pretend I hadn't been staring.

When I jerked my head to the side to avert my eyes, I swore I heard him chuckle, and as he passed me still sitting poolside, his fingertips grazed my shoulder and drifted across the back of my neck. Gooseflesh rose in their wake and my spine tingled. *That had to be on purpose,* I thought. But when I turned my head, all I saw was the back of him as he strode away towards the deep end of the pool.

***

He dove in, his lean frame cutting smoothly through the water, and emerged seconds later, shaking the water out of his hair. His muscular shoulders glistened in the sunlight, tiny droplets like little crystals of light pouring down his back.

I crossed my legs in an unconscious effort to contain the hot feeling pooling between them. I indulged in a little more shameless ogling before hauling myself up onto the paved pool side. I linked my fingers and stretched my arms high above my head, my muscles—warmed from my swim—extended in a palpable sensation of pleasure.

I closed my eyes to enjoy the stretch as best I could and when I opened them again, I was drawn to Billy's lithe form cutting through the water. I could've sworn he winked at me until he turned his head away again, alternating sides to breathe.

His form was impeccable, a perfect breaststroke borne from years spent in the water. Mine wasn't half bad either. One of the reasons we got along so well was our mutual love for the sport.

More and more I found myself imagining what lay beneath his swim trunks. What his muscles would feel like pressed against my own. Would his swimmers' legs lend to a different kind of experience? I was itching to find out.

Billy swam to the edge of the pool near where I stood and planted his hands on the side, pulling his beautiful body out in one smooth motion. Copying the same move I made earlier, he twisted mid air and planted himself on the edge of the pool. He glanced up at me, eyes crinkled against the suns bright light, his squint further exaggerated by his grin.

"Elle," he said, inclining his head. His coy smile betrayed the flirtatious intentions behind his innocent gesture, and I was glad none of the other lifeguards were near enough to feel the sexual energy crackling between us.

Deciding to throw caution to the wind and follow my instincts—which were rarely wrong when it came to men—I leant down, placing one hand delicately on his chiselled shoulder. "Twenty minutes until the pool opens," I whispered in his ear. "The pool house is empty." I trailed off suggestively, and when his head whipped around, his eyes met mine with a sparkle in them.

I slid my hand down his shapely bicep, not too obviously but enough to telegraph my intentions. I stood and slipped my fingers back up his arm, in a copy of the trail he had left across my neck and shoulders earlier. I hoped I was able to elicit the same response in his body as he had in mine. Then I walked towards the pool house, stopping only to let one of the other lifeguards know that Billy and I had some work to do in the office and would be back out momentarily.

As I crossed the threshold of the small building, I glanced back to see Billy looking idly around, trying to appear nonchalant as he followed my footsteps towards the door. I entered the office and backed up to the desk, perching myself delicately on the edge, waiting. He entered a moment later and closed the door behind him. He took in my position on the desk and grinned with delight, locking the door and moving to the other entrance to lock it as well.

***

He stalked towards me, a predator sizing up his *very* willing prey. Muscled sinew rippling beneath his skin as he moved lent to the stalking atmosphere he gave off with his movements and the expression that crossed his lovely face.

I was well aware now that his flirtations had been intentional, every step of the way. The hot feeling pooling between my thighs earlier that afternoon returned, intensified by his lustful stare as he approached me. I was eternally grateful that all that separated us was mere scraps of clothing and some air, because right now even the air was too much. It was all I could do to remain demure and wanting instead of doing what I wished I could, which was to rip through the spandex separating his most intimate parts from my own and join ourselves carnally.

He crossed the room, a lion stalking its gazelle, and I shifted my ass back onto the desk in anticipation. He stepped up between my legs—one hand on each kneecap—and gently spread them apart. I gasped, attempting to catch my breath. His hands slid up my bare legs from my knees to the delicate and sensitive skin of my inner thighs. As his thumbs skimmed close to the edge of my bathing suit I regained my boldness from before, reaching up and wrapping my arms around his neck, pulling his face to mine.

Our lips met—tentative at first—hesitant, feeling each other out. I ghosted my tongue across his lips, seeking entrance—which he willingly granted—and our distinct flavours mingled. A moan escaped my lips, swallowed by his own, as his hands moved upwards. My thighs felt bereft of touch as his fingers glided up my waist and around, seeking the bare skin exposed by the back of my suit. His fingertips slipped up my spine, leaving a trail of tingles in their wake.

I threaded the fingers of one hand through his soft, still wet hair. My other hand drifting down to the dip of his lower back to pull him closer, though still not close enough. I felt like he would never be close enough, not until he was inside me and maybe not even then. I kissed him like he was water and I hadn't had a drink in days, desperate and panting in between kisses. He returned my fervour equally with his own. I knew I hadn't been misinterpreting those signals from him!

He slipped the straps of my bathing suit off my shoulders, one at a time, and broke away from my mouth to drop soft kisses on each shoulder and up the side of my neck. I let my head drop back and focused on enjoying every feathery soft touch of his lips. I released him and leaned back on the desk, bracing myself with my hands.

He guided my bathing suit straps down my arms and I shimmied out of the top half. The cool air against my still damp skin make my nipples hard instantly. He must have noticed because he changed the direction of his kissing to trail down to one pert bud.

He took it in his mouth, and I moaned aloud.

"Shhhh,." Billy lifted his head to quiet me. "The others are still just outside, and I don't want to be interrupted before I've had my fill of you."

"Sorry," I replied, biting my lip to keep from crying out again as he resumed his task.

He gripped my waist with one hand, pulling me towards him with almost—but not quite—bruising force. With the other he palmed my breast that he wasn't currently lavishing attention on with his tongue. His rough hands caused jolts of pleasure from where he rubbed across my nipple right down to my aching core.

I decided after a few more delicious moments that I'd had enough of being a passive observer to our tryst. I wrapped my hands around his toned waist and dipped my fingers into the waistband of his swim trunks. Trailing them around the front, I teased the hem a little, then used one hand to rub his rock hard length through the damp fabric.

He gasped against my chest and tore his mouth away, the cool air a mild shock after the warmth I had been enjoying. He gripped the back of my neck, fingers tangling in my hair, and pulled me to him for a bruising kiss.

I placed both my hands firmly against his chest and pushed lightly, causing him to take a step back. I followed, refusing the break the kiss as I hopped off the desk I had been sitting on.

Once my feet were planted firmly on the floor I broke away long enough to yank my bathing suit the rest of the way off and step out of it. I followed his gaze as he looked my up and down, taking in my naked body in its entirety for the first time.

He grinned at me and followed my lead, dropping his trunks and kicking them to the side. "Back up on the desk," he said—no, he ordered—and I was quick to obey. He sank to his knees in front of me and spread mine apart. "I've been waiting to do this for so long." Without any more warning than that, he pressed his mouth against my core.

I choked off my cry of surprise and pleasure, biting down on my fist to suppress the noises I desperately wanted to make. His hot tongue ran up and down my slit before settling on my most sensitive spot. He flicked over my clit tirelessly, pushing me higher and higher towards sweet oblivion. With the hand I didn't have shoved against my mouth I reached out and grabbed the back of his head, holding on for dear life.

Hot, intense feelings of tightened in my belly, lower and seemingly all through my body. Like a spring waiting to be sprung I felt every muscle grow tighter and tighter. My grip on his hair increased in intensity as the sensations in my body crept closer and closer to overwhelming. Just when I thought I couldn't take it anymore, he plunged two fingers inside me and I exploded in a cascade of pleasure.

He moaned against my pussy, the vibrations only drawing my orgasm out further. He lapped up every drop and continued licking until I had stopped shaking from the intensity. When he stood, his erection must have been painfully hard by then. He pulled me off the desk on shaking legs.

I pressed against him for support, and claimed his lips with my own. I tasted myself on his tongue, it was not unpleasant and strangely arousing.

After a moment he pulled away. "I can't wait any longer," he panted.

Hooking his arms around my thighs, he lifted me up. I wrapped my legs around his waist instinctively and felt his hard cock press against my still throbbing center. He turned us and walked forward until my back came up against the cold wall.

I shivered at the sensation, in contrast to my skin that felt like it was on fire. I reached down between our bodies and lined him up with my sopping wet entrance, my flesh still tingling and tender from my orgasm thanks to his talented tongue.

Without hesitation, he thrust himself upwards, filling me up in one go. The stretch was delicious as my cunt seemed to form around him, a perfect fit. His strong hands gripped my ass, hard enough that I would probably have finger shaped bruises there later, but I was too far gone to care.

We'd also given up trying to be quiet, panting and moaning together as we lost ourselves to the sensation. I grabbed his shoulders and held on as he pounded into me. The wall behind me offering no resistance meant my body had to absorb the force.

Our coupling was frantic and full of desperate need. He slammed me into the unyielding surface hard and I pushed back harder with my hips, trying to take him as deep as I could over and over. As I reached the same peak as before and was about to tumble over, I released his shoulder with one hand and snaked it between us to find my aching, throbbing clit.

It was probably also bruised from the force of his thrusts and already sensitive. It didn't take long before I was throwing my head back, my mouth open but unable to make a sound as I rode wave after wave of ecstasy.

Billy followed my lead shortly after and groaned with one final, brutal thrust, his head dropping to my shoulder as he came hard. We stayed like that for a long moment, both us of leaning on the other, panting, desperate to catch our breath and gulp down some much-needed oxygen.

Eventually he lowered me to the ground, withdrawing from inside me with a soft hiss. My legs trembled and for a second I was sure I would collapse into a very satisfied puddle on the ground at his feet.

I looked around the office, our bathing suits laying discarded and half inside out on the floor. Papers and a few stationary supplies from the desk had also tumbled to the ground. *When did that even happen?* We'd been so caught up we hadn't even noticed, or at least I hadn't.

I looked up at the wall clock and gasped. "Shit! We have to get out there," I said, jerking my head towards the door as I snatched my bathing suit up off the ground. I jammed my feet into the leg holes and yanked it up. "Are you just going to stand there?" I asked, and reached up to snap my fingers in his face.

"Oh, right, no." He hastily stepped into his trunks and pulled them up, glancing at the clock himself as he did so. Once we were both clothed again, we took a moment to survey the mess surrounding us. As I sighed and started picking up papers off the floor, I heard Billy behind me chuckle.

"Maybe next time we do this at my place?"

"Next time?" I asked, straightening up and turning to stare. "I thought this was a one time, get our jollies off kind of thing?"

"Oh no," he said, his laughter intensifying, "if you think I'm not going to take every opportunity possible to do that again you're crazy." He plucked the paper from my hands and dropped it on the desk, then gripped my waist and pulled me towards him. I smiled and leaned up to place a quick kiss on his lips.

"Well, I'm definitely not crazy," I replied, "but next time, I vote we try and at least aim for somewhere softer than the wall."

"Deal."

END

Three

Devour Me

The music was so loud the walls vibrated with the bass beat that pounded through the hall of my dorm. October was drawing to a close and that meant it was party time, regardless of the fact that we weren't trick or treating anymore. If I'd learned anything in my three years at university it was that any excuse was a good excuse for a party. Halloween was as good a reason as any.

I finished applying my makeup using the small magnifying mirror set up on the side of my computer desk. Every inch of real estate was important in the tiny dorm rooms. So, my computer desk doubled as breakfast nook and vanity table when necessary. Little red riding hood was my costume of choice for this year. I expected to get my fair share of big bad wolf pick up lines tonight, but why else would I have picked this costume?

"Lauren!" someone called from the hallway, easy to hear since the door to my room stood wide open. Along with most of the doors in the hall. Parties like this tended to take place in and out of the small dorms. Turning the entire hall into one big party space for the night. If a door was closed it was safe to assume that it was occupied for—ahem—private activities and shouldn't be disturbed. The hallway was flooded with people in costume, every pop culture reference from the year mingling with all the holiday classics, and a few seriously questionable choices.

I finished up my make up and grabbed a cooler out of the tiny fridge in the corner of our room before heading out to join the party. I waded into the crowd, searching for the owner of the voice that had been calling for me, although it probably wasn't terribly important. More likely a friend wondering what was taking me so long. I liked to take my time getting done up, not for anyone else but because it made me feel good, it boosted my confidence and ability to interact with a bunch of half in the bag frat boys.

I used my concert maneuvering skills to make my way through the crowd, elbows out and walk sideways. I only made it about 15 feet before I was accosted by Emma, my roommate. "Lauren!" she practically screamed in my ear. "Your costume is fucking awesome hun!" She tried to wrap her arm around my shoulders but actually ended up hooking it around my neck, I leaned into it and slugged back my cooler. I was clearly behind in the drinking department.

Emma was dressed in a store-bought French maid costume, not the most original but who was I to judge? She looked amazing in it and her chestnut locks were curled to perfection, bouncing around her shoulders defying gravity. I would pay money to learn how to use a curling iron like she could. My own pin straight hair—recently dyed fire engine red—at least matched my own costume. That was the closest I was going to get to a good hair style, but it was easy to brush so I'll take what I can get.

I tipped my head back for another deep swallow of my drink as Emma tightened her grip on my neck. "I have a present for you," she half whispered half yelled in my ear. I laughed and pulled myself free before she pulled me any closer or strangle my right here in the hallway by accident.

"Present?" I asked with a raised eyebow.

"Yes!" she said and pressed a finger to her mouth, "shhhh!"

"Emma…" I started slowly, "what is the present?"

"Oh! Hold on," she replied and suddenly she pulled away from me entirely and grabbed the shoulder of a guy nearby dressed as what I guessed was some kind of animal. "Lauren! This is Mark, Mark this is Lauren," she said as she spun him around to face me. "Look, he's a wolf… red riding hood and the wolf, get it?" Emma collapsed into giggles, releasing Marks shoulder in the process. He was kind enough to catch her and make sure she didn't hit the ground on the questionable dorm hall carpet. Together we guided her over to a near chair. Once Emma was safely seated with a table beside her for her drink I turned to the aforementioned Mark.

"I am so sorry, thank you for not laughing in her face." I said.

"What and become the worlds biggest hypocrite?" he replied, "like she's the first person to drink too much at a dorm party."

"That's refreshing," I said with a sigh of relief, I tipped my cooler back and finished it off.

"Can I get you another drink?" Mark asked as he took the empty bottle from my hand.

"That would be excellent," I said with a dip of my head, "just another cooler would be perfect, and maybe a water for Emma."

"Done," he replied and waded into the crowd. I hovered around Emma who had sunk into the chair and was giggling at something on her phone.

"Hey! Check this out," she yelled—even though I was approximately 8 inches away—and held out her phone wobbling it in front of my face. I reached out and steadied her hand in order to see the meme she was trying to show me, which was pretty funny to be fair. I was still chuckling to myself and guiding the phone back to her lap without her dropping it when Mark came back with a cooler for me and a red solo cup of water for Emma.

"Thank you so much," I said taking the two drinks from him. I leaned over Emma and pressed the solo cup into her free hand, "hey hun, drink this for me eh?"

"Hmm?" she mumbled as she gripped the cup a little too hard, "yeah, mhmm." Noncommittal as her response was, she did bring it to her lips and chug back half the water before she even realized it wasn't alcoholic. She grimaced, but continued to drink it, satisfied that she was safely hydrating herself for the moment I turned my attention back to the handsome wolf.

"Thanks again," I said, inclining my bottle towards him in a mock cheers before chugging back a quarter of the bottle.

"No problem," he replied, taking a deep slug of his beer. "I think now I'm supposed to say something so cheesy it could almost be cute but is actually just embarrassing, but I can't think of anything that doesn't start with a red riding hood joke."

"Oh, I came prepared for red riding hood jokes, here I'll even start one for you…my what big teeth you have Mr. Wolf." I said smiling up at him.

"The better to eat you with my…" Mark trailed off and doubled over with laughter, "I can't," he gasped, "I can't even say that with a straight face."

When I recovered from our terrible attempt at red riding hood related pick up lines I turned to check on Emma, who had finished her water and was scrolling her phone in the chair looking much more clear-eyed. I nudged her with my ankle to get her attention and she looked for a moment, raised her eyebrows and then nodded enthusiastically and went back to her phone. Drunk or not my girl has always got my back. I took the hint that she was ok, and I could continue flirting with my 'present'.

***

"So Mark, I love a bad pick up line as much as the next girl," I said. *Pulling out all the cliché stops tonight.* "But would you be interested in an actual conversation? Somewhere that we can actually hear ourselves think?" I asked, eyelashes fluttering.

"What did you have in mind?" He replied, reaching his hand for mine and just brushing against the back of my fingers. The tingles that lingered there were enough for me to follow through with my original thought.

"Well, my room is just a few doors down the hall." I said with a wink and cocked my head towards my dorm.

"I like the sound of that," Mark said as he flashed me a gorgeous smile. *Oh yeah, good choice Emma!* I made a mental note to thank my roomie in the morning for her good taste. And if things continued heading in the direction I hoped they were heading, I'd also have to thank her for finding another place to crash tonight.

I turned towards my room and grabbed Mark's hand to lead him through the crowd. The people had begun to thin out, less crowd control moves were necessary to make our way back to my door. When we reached it, I gestured inside for Mark to lead the way; he raised an eyebrow but didn't say anything as he stepped inside. I made an executive decision and shut the door behind us, surreptitiously clicking the lock behind my back. He looked back at me as the lock clicked behind my back and grinned. *Definitely the right decision.*

"Wow," Mark said, looking around the tiny room. "I'd forgotten how tiny these dorm rooms are. I moved off campus after first year."

"I've thought about it," I replied, "but I like the whole community aspect of living right here on campus, plus I don't have to cook or clean a kitchen living here." I laughed.

It became apparent that he was casting about for somewhere to sit but didn't want to be so presumptuous as to sit on the bed. I decided to help him out and sit there myself, hoping he would take the hint. He did—much to my delight—and quickly sat down beside me. I made the split-second decision to skip the awkward fumbling and leaned over to press my lips to his.

He responded fervently and slipped one hand around the back of my neck and immediately became tangled in the hood of my cape. I couldn't stop the giggle that bubbled up in my throat and pulled back from the kiss.

"Let's get this out of the way shall we?" I asked and reached for the ties on looped loosely at my neck.

"Hold on, let me." Mark replied and gently tugged on the fabric to release the knot. He slipped the cape off my shoulders and I lifted myself off the mattress just enough for him to tug the whole thing free and drop it unceremoniously to the floor. "Where were we?" He said with a wink.

"Apparently still in the land of cheesy one liners," I replied with a cheeky grin and he pulled me forward for a hard, passionate kiss. I moaned against his lips and he obligingly opened them to grant access to my desperate tongue. He tasted like the cheap beer most dorm parties had in abundance, but I was too distracted by the sensual feeling of his tongue against mine to care. Eventually, when oxygen started to become an issue I pulled back and took a deep gulp of air.

"Left you breathless, did I?" He asked smiling.

"You know, you talk entirely too much for a big bad wolf, aren't you supposed to be trying to devour me?" I replied, eyebrow raised.

"As you wish my dear," he said, his voice suddenly dropping an octave and sending shivers down my spine. My cape was already discarded on the floor, leaving me in a red tank top with matching skirt and black knee-high boots, my bare legs exposed in between. Mark both hands firmly on my shoulders and pushed until I was laying back on the bed. He shifted back far enough to guide my legs up as well, tapped the side of my boot as he did so, "I like these, they can stay," he said. Warmth pooled in my belly as he slid his hands up my thighs under my skirt quickly finding the bare scrap of red lace panties I had on underneath.

I reached out to run my hands up his muscled arms. "Ah, ah," he said and gently eased my arms back down, "I'm doing the devouring remember?" He trailed his fingers along the hemline of panties under my skirt before gently trailing them down my legs, easing them over my boots and discarding them to join my cape on the floor. My skin tingled with goosebumps where he touched me and it was very hard to keep my hands to myself, but I was intrigued by this game we were apparently playing with each other.

He spread my knees as wide as they would go and settled himself comfortably between my legs, pushing my skirt up around my hips and exposing my most intimate part to him and the slightly chill air. He leaned down and blew ever so gently against my clit, the sensation of cool air intensifying made me gasp in surprise and pleasure. He gently put his hands around my wrists, pinning my arms to the bed on either side of me, pausing for just a moment to look up and raise a questioning eyebrow, I nodded enthusiastically in response and he finally dipped his head down to my pussy, and began the aforementioned devouring.

The warmth of his tongue right after being exposed to the cool air sent shockwaves radiating through my body from my core. His skillfully swirled his tongue around my slit, up and down occasionally dipping in but very studiously avoiding my clitoris. Within moments my legs were trembling with need and my hips lifted of the bed, desperate for more contact. I still couldn't move my arms as he held them steadfastly against the mattress, it was both frustrating and incredibly hot. I tossed my head from side to side and let out a low moan that was half pleased and half wanting. He decided to take pity on my plight at that moment and flicked his tongue across my clit with what felt like in human speed, releasing one of my wrists to slide two fingers into my sopping entrance at the same time.

The orgasm that tore through me was like fire bursting from the inside out, I used my now free hand to grab my pillow and press it over my face to muffle the scream of ecstasy that tore its way out of my throat. He kept going and going, my hips thrusting up against his face until I collapsed against the mattress, and heap of satisfied limbs unable to move as I currently couldn't feel my extremities.

***

"Sufficiently devoured?" Mark asked, pulling the pillow away from my face and pressing his lips to my neck, then my earlobe and finally my mouth. Now his kisses tasted like the musky scent of my own orgasm, which only served to reignite the flames of desire inside me. I gripped the back of his neck and kissed him back, hard. Then I reached for the nightstand drawer, fumbling around as I was unwilling to break of our delicious kiss in order to see what I was doing. Finally, I found the handle and wrenched the drawer open. Mark broke off the kiss at the sound and looked over, then smiled down at me and propped himself up on one arm so he could reach for a little foil square inside the drawer.

I tugged on the bottom of his shirt while he did so, running one hand up underneath and over the planes of his abs. He obliged me and leaned back on his ankles and pulled it off over his head, dislodging his wolf mask that I hadn't even noticed was pushed back on his head. I removed my own tank top in response, revealed the red lace bra that matched my previously discarded underwear. I leaned up on my elbows to unhook my bra, but he reached out to stop me, "ooh no leave that on," he said his tone low and slightly commanding.

I obeyed and lay back on the bed, "Yessir," I replied with a grin.

"Good girl," he growled at me, and stood for a brief moment to discard his pants. He slipped them off and stared down at me laid out on the bed. My hair was a mess I was sure, make up smudged with just my bra on and a red skirt bunched up around my hips, my knee-high boots still in place."God, you are gorgeous," he said. I blushed in response as he returned to the bed and crawled slowly up my body.

"You're not so bad yourself," I replied when he was eye level with me again. He pressed his lips to my gently and one hand skimmed up the curve of my waist before brushed against one lace covered nipple causing me to gasp at the unexpected sensation. I arched my back, pressing my breast against his palm as he continued to rub against it. The rough feeling of the lace over my taut nipple was different but not unpleasant, my eyes drifted closed as he lowered his mouth to my neck and kissed his way down one side then across my chest and back up the other.

I heard the rip of foil and opened my eyes again as he lined himself up at my entrance. I was so wet from his ministrations that he slid in easily despite his size, I reveled in the delicious stretch as my internal muscles adjusted to accommodate him. He stayed very still for a moment, graciously giving my time to adjust. Which I appreciated but very quickly found myself desperate for friction, I gripped his hips and thrust mine upwards to encourage him.

"Needy aren't you?" He said, still not moving as I writhed beneath him.

"Less talking and more fucking please Mr. Wolf." I replied with a moan.

"Since you asked so nicely," he said, as he braced his arms on the either side of my head and suddenly began pounding me into the mattress. I gripped his shoulder hard with one hand and had to reach for my pillow once again to muffle my screams as drove his hard cock deep inside me. Hitting that perfect spot each time that pushed me closer and closer to the edge of oblivion.

I was surely leaving marks on this shoulder, but we were both too lost in the feeling of each other to care. I jerked my hips up to meet him thrust for the thrust and the top of my bed hit the wall with each movement, distantly in the very recesses of my mind I was glad there was still a party going on and hoped other people would mistake the slamming of the headboard for the bassline of the music.

He reached for my chest once again, pinching my straining nipple through the red lace and I tipped over the edge he had been pushing me to. Fireworks exploded behind my eyes and my thrusting became increasingly erratic, unable to keep pace as the orgasm wracked my body drawing out longer than it should have been possible. Every nerve ending tingled and I dimly realized I wasn't the only one becoming slightly erratic as Mark groaned low in his throat, sounding every inch the big bad wolf for a moment and he came.

He dropped on top of my and we lay sweating and panting in a tangle of limbs for a moment trying to remember how to breathe evenly once again. He pulled out of me once we were both able to move again and rolled beside me on the small bed.

"Remind me in the morning to buy Emma some flowers," he said.

"She's allergic actually, but you can split with me on the giant box of chocolates I'm going to get for her." I replied. We laughed and I leaned in for a quick kiss, "Do I get to have a turn doing the devouring?" I asked.

"Absolutely," he replied his eyes lighting up, "tomorrow, after I remember how to move my legs."

"Deal," I said and laid my head against his shoulder for some much-needed sleep.

END

Four

House Call

"Goddammit!" I cursed under my breath as I limped my way into the hospital emergency room. *Well done Alexa, fuck up your ankle right before your first week on the new job.* I couldn't have been more pissed at myself. Why did I think that a date at a skating rink was a good idea? The single life was getting old.

I was tired of the same old coffee houses and local bars. So, when my latest Tinder match suggested ice skating, I was super excited. Even though I'm a terrible skater. I figured I could fake till I make it, sort of. I've skated before, I'm not a total novice. But I thought, you know if I'm falling down clumsy, he'll help me. *That's attractive right? Dudes wanna help the damsel in distress.*

Unfortunately, he apparently had the same idea. So, we stumbled around together until I did something awful to my ankle and had to bail. He didn't even offer to help me into the

ER, just dropped me off at the door.

Sigh, why am I incapable of picking dudes who treat me like a human being instead of just a penis receptacle? I hopped my way over to the triage check in and fished my health card out of my purse.

"How can I help you today?" Sitting behind the triage desk was quite possibly the most beautiful man I had ever seen. I tried to contain my swoon as I slid my health card across the desk.

"I fu-screwed up my ankle," I said, biting back the curse word at the last moment in an attempt to not sound like a sailor.

"I can see that," he said with a cheeky grin. "Why don't you take a seat and get your weight off it while I take down your info?"

"Awesome," I replied with a sigh as I sank into the chair.

He took down my information and checked it against my digital health record. All the while I tried to distract myself from the throbbing pain in my ankle by ogling my sexy nurse, imagining what might be hidden under those scrubs.

"So, the doc is gonna be a little while. My unprofessional opinion is that you have a sprained ankle, but I can't say for sure." He slid my health card back to me under the plastic partition that protected the triage team from germs.

"Unprofessional? Aren't you a medical professional? You work in a hospital," I replied with a skeptically raised eyebrow.

"Yes, I am. Sort of." He flashed that cheeky grin again and continued, "If you promise not to sue, I'll tell you a trade secret."

I blinked at him and glanced around. I wasn't holding up the line—there was no one else waiting to triage at the moment.

"Ok, I promise, spill," I demanded. Every second of our conversation was further distraction from the pain in my ankle that was currently progressing further and further up my lower leg.

"Well," he started, "I am a medical professional, technically. In that I went to school and have certificates and all that. In fact, I'm probably more qualified to diagnose simple things like a sprained ankle better than most doctors in this hospital."

"Simple?" I asked, incredulous. "I'm in a lot of pain you know!"

"Of course, I do!" he replied quickly. "I mean simple case wise, as in you don't have a complex medical disorder that requires months or years of in-depth treatment."

"Sorry," I cut in quickly before he could continue, "it just hurts a lot and I'm a baby."

"You're not a baby," he said, reaching through the plastic partition to hold my hand momentarily. "Sprains are a bitch. But as I was saying, most of the doctors around here spend so much time on more serious cases that these simple triage solvable issues are handled by us nurses. Usually what happens is we do the intake, we tell the patient that we can't say what the problem is, and then we tell the doc what we think it is."

"And you're always right?" I asked.

"I wouldn't say always," he said with a barely noticeable wink. "But usually."

In spite of the pain in my leg I smiled back at him. "Thanks nurse…?"

"You can just call me Mark," he replied. "I'll bring your paperwork to the back, it shouldn't be too long." He flashed that grin at me again and I told myself that the tingles I felt were due to my body's reaction to my ankle and not my body reacting to Mark's stunning smile. *C'mon now Alexa, the hot nurse is probably exhausted by the idea of patients hitting on him.*

Let's try and contain the hormones girl.

Mark disappeared from view around the mint green walls that all hospitals seem to have. I sat back in the hard, plastic chair and waited, slightly impatiently. True to his word, he was back in just a few moments.

"Alright," he said, glancing down at my paperwork, "Alexa. I'm going to take you in the back and get you set up for an x-ray. The doc wants to check for any breakage."

"Ok," I replied, and stood with a wince. I hobbled past the triage desk and followed Mark down the hallway. Past the wall he had previously disappeared behind was the bustling active center of the ER department. Several more nurses moved quickly back and forth between rows of hospital beds that were sectioned off with privacy curtains. We continued around the corner until he opened the door of the x-ray room.

"I'm gonna need you to hop up on the table here, and put your leg out straight," he said, gesturing to the paper covered hospital bed in front of us.

"Uhm, I'll try," I said with a dubious glance at the bed's height.

"Here, let me help you." Mark wrapped one arm around my back for support. I leaned into him and hoisted myself up. His hand was so warm against my waist I could feel it even through my shirt.

I tried to ignore the thoughts that floated through my pervy brain. *I wonder how those hands would feel somewhere else?* On second thought, I almost never come to the hospital, I'll probably never see this guy again. Why not indulge a little fantasy? It would definitely help take my mind off things.

I wiggled my butt across the bed until I could get my leg straight out in front of me. *Is it my imagination or is he holding on a little bit too long?* Mark's face was very close to mine, and I couldn't stop myself from turning towards him. We made eye contact for just a second and it felt like someone had electrified the air. He felt it too—at least I thought he did—and broke contact first, straightening up and awkwardly clearing his throat.

I cast about for anything else to focus on that wasn't his gorgeous eyes, or impossibly good-looking face. I settled for staring at my own injured leg, which I had completely forgotten about despite the obvious swelling.

Mark wheeled the portable x-ray machine across the room and set it up over the top of my busted ankle. It clicked and whirred, making unsettling noises that offered a welcome reprieve from my blood pounding in my ears. My wandering eyes, however, drifted back to my attentive nurse.

His scrub pants were just a little too tight around his hips, showing off his shapely ass and thighs. I stared unabashedly for a couple more minutes and when I glanced up again, he was watching me with not-quite-concealed smirk.

My cheeks flamed with embarrassment at being caught openly ogling my nurse, but I couldn't help but notice he was distinctly unbothered by it. In fact, he appeared to be into it, if the very un-nurse-like way his eyes lingered over my own body was any indication.

Alexa, really? The super hot guy is checking you out while x-raying your ankle? Daydream much?

"We're all set here," he said, breaking through my self-deprecating thoughts. "I have to have a real doctor look at the images." He chuckled. "But I should be back soon to help you wrap that up. Pretty sure there won't be any casts involved."

"Thanks." I watched him walk out the door and just before he closed it, he turned back and winked at me. *Omigod he is flirting with me!* I was left alone with my thoughts, trying to wrap my head around how I ended up in this situation. Just an hour ago I was a bad first date, and now I was getting hit on—subtly—by the sexiest nurse I'd ever seen outside of a medical drama show. *What do I do now? Try and slip him my number?* He would probably be way to professional to respond to something like that. *But not too professional to wink at me,* I reminded myself.

Well, if I was giving out my number to dudes on Tinder who couldn't even be bothered to help me into the hospital when I hurt myself, why couldn't I give it to the flirtatious nurse who *did* help me?

It took awhile for Mark to get back from consulting with the doctor. Presumably because the doc was busy helping fix up real patients, not morons who sprained their ankle trying to do a sport they're not good at.

This gave me ample time to work up my courage, and also dig around in my bag for a pen and paper. I didn't have a notepad but what I did have was a terrible receipt hoarding habit. I checked them all, trying to find the least objectionable one. Something I wouldn't mind him knowing that I had bought when he inevitably turned it over and read the other side.

He came back in with my x-ray results, those sheets that look like giant photo negatives.

"Good news!" he said with a wide grin. "I was right—not to toot my own horn—and you just have a sprain." He produced a tensor bandage from his pocket. "We'll get you wrapped up and the best thing you can do is stay off of it as much as possible, elevate and ice it to help with the swelling. Over the counter pain meds should help, but don't over do it. Follow the dosage instructions on the bottle, ok?"

"I think I can handle some run of the mill painkillers," I replied with a matching grin of my own. "Glad to hear I'm not broken."

Moving to the end of my bed, he gently took my ankle in his hands and slid my leggings up out of the way. I sucked in my breath with a hiss, gritting my teeth though the pain caused by movement.

"Sorry, I'll try to be gentle, but speedy," he said, glancing up at me.

"It's ok," I said with a reassuring smile, "I'm a big girl, I can take it."

True to his word, he quickly wrapped up my ankle and our chance encounter was rapidly coming to an end. *Now or never.* I swung my legs off the bed and scooped up my purse. I clutched the receipt with my number on it.

I limped my way towards the doorway and paused in the opening. I glanced back over my shoulder—mirroring his earlier actions—and hoped he would pick up the hint. I made very deliberate eye contact and winked.

Mark's eyes widened a fraction and looked down at my closed fist. I released the receipt on the desk beside the door. I left as quickly as I was able after that, fingers internally crossed, and a self-satisfied smirk firmly planted on my lips.

***

Enough days passed that my ankle was starting to feel substantially better, and I had pretty much given up hope of hearing from Mark. It was a long shot; he'd probably be crossing some professional lines to call or text a patient. But I was still glad I had done it.

I let myself into my apartment after work, grateful for the weekend and cursing my building's lack of an elevator at the same time. My phone trilled out a text message notification from inside my purse as I unlocked the door while standing on one foot. I could feel the tensor bandage slipping down my ankle, loose from walking around during the day and then hopping my way up three flights of stairs.

"Hold on, hold on," I said out loud to no one as my phone went off again. *Key in lock and turn, don't fall down. I'm getting pretty good at this.* I made it through the door and dropped my keys in the dish on the table. A few more hops and I collapsed gracelessly onto the couch. I propped my injured foot up on the pillow that had found a new semi permanent home on my coffee table, ignoring the loose bandage for now. I'd just have to take it off to shower soon anyways. I dug my phone out of my purse and blinked at the message on the screen, unable to process what I was seeing for a solid minute.

The message on my lock screen was from a number I didn't know. It started: *Hey, this is super unprofessional, but I haven't been able to...*the preview cut off the rest.

My heart pounding, I tapped the screen to open the rest of the message...*stop thinking about you. I assume you left this number for a reason. Would you want to get together some time? – Mark*

Holy shit. I couldn't believe what I was reading. I had pretty much written off any chance of him contacting me. Did I want to get together sometime? What does that mean, coffee, dinner, crazy fun sexy times? *Please, please be the last one.*

I hesitated, thumbs poised over my keyboard, and tried to think of a flirty response. *Hey Mark,* I typed out, *you assume correctly. I'd love to get together sometime, but I'm not doing a lot of walking around these days.*

I put my phone facedown on my lap and sat, tapping my fingers, impatiently waiting for a response. Within seconds, the telltale sound rang out, and my phone vibrated against my thigh.

I'd be more than willing to do a relaxing, sitting down activity with you lol. His text made me smile and I decided to throw caution to the wind. I'd already given my phone number out to my nurse after all.

How about a popcorn and movie on my couch? I have Netflix. I would never in my life use the phrase Netflix and Chill, but I figured that I could still get the idea across.

His response, *Sure! Tonight?* came back so fast I was glad to see I wasn't the only eager party here. I sent him back my address and told him to give me an hour before coming. *See you soon!* accompanied by a winking smiley came back, once again at lightning speed.

I headed for the shower as quickly as I could, my loose tensor bandage finally slipping off my ankle to the floor as I went.

I checked my phone as I stepped out of the shower, trying not to drip on the screen. *35 minutes to go.* I hurried—as fast as possible in my semi crippled state—to my room and tried to find something passably sexy to wear. By the time I was dressed and half blow-drying half brushing my hair, there was a knock at the door.

"Just a sec," I called and dashed on some eyeliner and lipstick. Not too fancy, but enough to make it look like I put some effort into my appearance. I made my way to the door, and paused momentarily to catch my breath. I peeked through the peephole and there he was. Even more heart stopping dressed in casual clothes, he had a small bouquet of flowers in his hands. I tried to contain my swoon at his thoughtfulness and opened the door.

"Hi there," Mark said as he passed the threshold, "these are for you, I hope you're not allergic." He handed me the flowers and cocked his head with a questioning smile playing on his lips.

"Thanks." I nodded in response. "I'm not. Make yourself comfortable while I find a vase, which is actually code for tallest glass I own."

Mark laughed lightly in response to my poor joke and made his way to the couch in my living room, smiling at my pillow prop on the coffee table.

Heading back from the kitchen, I tried to plan out what my move was here—I'm not the most seductive human. See above, my horrible ice-skating plan and subsequent failure. I needn't have worried though, as I sat on the couch next to him Mark placed a light hand on my thigh.

"How's your ankle feeling?"

"Oh, good," I replied, "much better, actually."

"That's good," he said, "I was worried." And then he kissed me.

Shocked for a second, I just blinked, but when he slipped his hand tenderly around the back of my neck, my eyes drifted closed and I parted my lips in response to soft kisses. His hand on my thigh slipped up around my waist and he pulled me tight against him. I could feel the hard planes of his abs muscles pressed against my stomach and I wound my own hands around his shoulders.

We responded to each other with equal ease and eagerness, desperate to explore, but somehow it also felt natural, like we had done this a thousand times together. After a few moments he pulled away, leaving me gasping for oxygen and bereft of his touch.

"I'm sorry," he said, "but I've been dreaming about that for two weeks."

"I've been dreaming about even more," I replied, surprised by my own boldness. I reached for the bottom of his shirt and tugged it up over his head before leaning in to capture his lips again. He responded with equal fervour, breaking the kiss only to remove and toss my own shirt away. It didn't take us long to divest each other of the rest of our clothes and shift our way into a comfortable horizontal position on the couch. As he lay between my thighs—the sheer lace of my panties the only thing separating us—his arousal was increasingly obvious.

He slipped a hand between us as he kissed his way down my neck and across my collarbone. When his fingers parted me and slipped gently inside, my head fell back against the arm of the couch as sounds of ecstasy escaped my lips. I could feel Mark's grin against the tender skin at the hollow of my throat and then the soft touch of his fingers skating across my breast. Goosebumps followed the wake left by his fingers, even though my skin felt like he was leaving a trail of fire instead.

His fingers inside me pumped in and out, curved in just the right way, urging me closer and closer to the edge. His mouth found its way back to mine and as he flicked his thumb over my clit I arched into his hand, shockwaves of pleasure radiating out from my center. He slowed his ministrations but didn't stop immediately, easing me down from the peaks I had reached. Once I had regained the ability to form coherent thoughts, I reached between us and grasped his hard length, sliding my hand up and down until he moaned into my mouth and I could feel his breathing quicken as he broke off the kiss and leaned his forehead against my shoulder.

He stopped my hand and gripped my hips with his, gently shifting my position on the couch until one leg was braced against the floor. He knelt between my thighs and reached for something on the floor. My eyes drifted closed as he palmed one breast, fingers pinching my taut nipple, then I heard the tell-tale tear of foil. I opened my eyes again to watch and he looked at me intently, waiting for confirmation. In response to my nod he leaned forward again and eased himself inside.

I lifted my hips to match his rhythm and we moved in time with one another, slowly, exploring each sensation and feeling. He held me against him—one hand on my lower back and one at the back of my neck—as he worshiped my lips, face and neck with soft open-mouthed kisses. My orgasm came on suddenly, I'd been so wrapped up the feel of him that I didn't even notice until my thighs started to shake. He picked up his pace, thrusting faster and faster until he joined me tumbling over the edge, his cock buried deep inside me.

I wasn't sure how long we laid on the couch after that, eventually he lifted himself off me and disappeared to find a garbage can. He returned with a glass of water and my tensor bandage.

I laughed out loud. "You've caught me neglecting my after care," I said.

"Well, I'll just have to stick around and take care of you myself then," he replied. Since I still hadn't moved, and had absolutely no desire to yet, he settled back down on the couch beside me as we basked in the afterglow. Eventually he did wrap up my ankle again, if only to make it stable enough for us to relocate to the bedroom.

We never even turned on Netflix.

END

Five

Private Lessons

orking out is such a pain in the ass. I hate it, but I'm also shallow. Oh and there's that whole health thing too, right? I want to like it. I see people in yoga class who don't look like they're dying, they must be enjoying themselves. Or they are better actors than me. I don't have the concentration to get through the workout and hide my pain at the same time.

It was with all this in mind that when my yoga class finished its run and I had to pick something else. I went with the kick boxing class. The class that had the absolute hottest instructor in the gym. Possibly the hottest man in the whole town. I don't know, I haven't seen them all. But damn.

I figured the eye candy would help me get through the workout induced torture. Except now, I was facing a whole new problem. My desperate and all-consuming need to bone my instructor.

I said that I was shallow right? I have needs like any other woman, and I so badly wanted that man to fulfill those needs. Repeatedly and at length, preferably over a long weekend near a beach, but I'm not picky.

So now, my concentration is split three ways. Power through the workout, attempt to hide my hatred for working out, and hide my lady boner. It's more difficult when I keep putting myself front and centre in the class, so I can better see the moves, not so I can ogle the instructor! So, I'm shallow and I lie to myself, sue me. At least I'm honest. Wait.

My next class is later this week and I've decided to embrace the lady boner. He doesn't have a ring on his finger which leaves at least the possibility that he might be single. That's what I have to work with. I need help in the worst way.

I've decided to call in the big guns, my best friend Isabella, an expert at seduction and sex. I spent most of my twenties in a monogamous relationship—not a great one I'll admit—but while I was wasting my time, Bella was experiencing the best of all worlds; variety. Men, women, et cetera. Since I am woefully ignorant of how people flirt nowadays, I have no choice but to follow her plan, whatever it may be.

"So, you wanna bone the hot kickboxer guy?" Isabella asked as she set a steaming cup of coffee on the table in front of me and took a seat.

I chuckled as I wrapped my hands around the oversized mug in an attempt to warm some feeling back into them. Another reason I attend gym classes that suck the money out of my wallet instead of running for free in the park is the fact that the weather isn't always cooperative. Especially during the winter when the snow is knee deep and the air hurts my face. And also evidently, my fingers. I should've worn gloves on my walk to

Isabella's apartment, but I like to pretend it's not as cold as it really is. Denial makes me feel better, but alas, not warmer.

"Yes, to put it in the crudest way possible, I wanna bone the kickboxer guy. I bow before your superior sexiness and knowledge. Teach me, wise one." I barely got the last sentence out before bursting into giggles.

Bella had more composure but only long enough to say,"I will teach you my ways grasshopper." She then doubled over and we spent a solid few minutes laughing until we gasped for air and wiped away tears.

"Make fun of me all you want," I said. "I came to you in good faith, looking for advice, asshat."

"Call me asshat one more time and I refuse to help you get the D." Isabella said with a smirk.

"Ok, ok." I held my hands up in mock surrender. "I bow to your experience and expertise."

"Damn right you do!" Bella said with a smirk. "If you want my advice, I feel like you already know what it is."

"I don't," I replied with a confused frown.

"Yes, you do," she said. "You have to put on your big girl pants and ask the dude to bone you."

"I can't do that!"

"Why the hell not? Worst case scenario, he says no and you are exactly where you are now. With the exact same level of negative dick. Best case scenario, however, is you get to be on the positive dick side of the equation, and you get to fulfil a fantasy."

"What so I just wander up after class, sweaty and disgusting, and go 'hey wanna stick it in?'" I scrunched up my face to further illustrate my distaste for her idea.

"Oh my god, Taylor, no." Isabella laughed in my face, in a

nice I'm-your-best-friend-so-I-can-do-this-to-you way. "I'll tell you what to do but let me get us more coffee first." With that declaration, she stood and headed for the kitchen. I slumped forward, leaning my head heavily into my hands. *What have I gotten myself into?*

***

It took me two more weeks to work up the nerve to even consider doing what Isabella told me to do. Two more painfully sex-deprived weeks. Of course, Bella has taken every opportunity to make fun of me for procrastinating. But let's be real, I would totally do the same to her. I'm sure I have in the past for a variety of reasons. That's what friends do right?

So, the big girl pants took a while to put on, but if I put it off any more, I'm going to explode from sexual tension and that'll just be unpleasant for everyone involved.

We reached the cooldown portion of the class, and I was epically grateful for the chance to let some of the sweat evaporate. The less gross I look, the better my chances of scoring. My mind raced with instructions as I went through the movements I had memorized from several weekly classes already. The class ended and I took a deep breath to steady my nerves on my way to the side of the room where we all threw our bags.

Be obvious, but not desperate, Isabella had said. I reached into the pocket of my purse as I approached the front of the room and fished out the piece of paper inside.

"Hi, Brandon, right?" I said, even though I already knew.

"Yeah," he replied, "what's up?" He looked me up and down in the not-at-all subtle way guys have of moving their eyes but not their heads. Do they really think that we don't notice? In this case I was totally ok with it, since I had been objectifying and undressing him in my mind for weeks. Fair is fair after all.

"I was wondering if you would be available for some *private* lessons?" I asked, putting as much emphasis on private as I dared with people still slowly milling out of the room around us. As I did, I boldly slipped the piece of paper from my purse into his hand and flashed a winning, flirtatious smile.

Don't give him time to answer right away, was another of Bella's instructions. So, I withdrew my hand from his, batted my eyelashes suggestively at his look of surprised confusion and walked away, making sure to swing my hips just a little bit more than usual. At the doorway, I stopped and glanced back over my shoulder. Brandon was just looking up from the note paper which contained my cell phone number.

He grinned at me and winked, and I damn near passed out, so I stepped around the doorframe to lean on the outside wall. Mission accomplished.

I buzzed with excitement and dread all afternoon. This is fucking crazy. I can't believe I straight up handed him my number and asked him for private lessons. The internal beratement went on for quite a while until I was jolted by my phone vibrating in my back pocket.

Ohgodohgodohgod. I jabbed the messaging app icon harder than was strictly necessary in my excitement slash nervousness. The message that popped up was just as flirty and suggestive as I hoped I had been earlier that day.

I typed out a quick response with shaky fingers. Get a grip Taylor, jesus, it's just a hot dude and potentially awesome sex. Of course, it could also be potentially awful sex. That thought sobered me a little, enough to calm the hell down.

Within a few minutes of text exchange, enough for both of us to confirm that we were thinking the same thing, I sent him my address and practically ran to the shower.

Less than an hour later, I was clean, shaved, and smelling delicious. Ready for my private lessons with Brandon. I poured myself half a glass of wine, enough for a little liquid courage but not so much as to impair my judgement.

I had already double checked my side table for all the goodies, lube, condoms etc. All well stocked up. My phone buzzed on the table—in true millennial fashion, Brandon had texted to signal his arrival rather than just knocking on the door. I shot back a quick text to say come on up, and tried to look like I wasn't panting with anticipation when he walked through the door.

He stepped through the doorway looking much different than I was used to seeing him. In a very very good way. He had swapped his workout clothes for tight fitting jeans and a silk button up over a black t-shirt, further solidifying that he was picking up what I was putting down, if you know what I mean. We definitely weren't going to be doing any kickboxing with him dressed like that. In a perfect world, he soon wouldn't be dressed at all.

"Hello," I said, trying not to sound like a moron. How do you greet your gym instructor/booty call? Is there a memo on that somewhere that I missed?

"Hi." Brandon smiled, and thankfully seemed to be having the same awkward 'how do we get from here to nakedness' thoughts that I was.

Well fuck it, let's just jump right in, shall we? I walked across the room to where he stood just inside the door and attempted to muster up all the confidence I could.

"Thanks for coming," I said with a flirty smile, and pressed my lips to his.

***

For a half a second he didn't respond, shocked I assumed by my boldness but who are we kidding? We both know why he's here. Then the floodgates seemed to open.

He wrapped his strong arms around me, one hand on the small of my back and the other lightly gripping my neck and spun us both around until I was pressed against the door. I moaned into his mouth as he took charge of the situation, which gave him the opportunity to deepen the kiss I had started.

I slipped my hands up underneath his shirt, slowly running my fingers along the ridges of abs and around his waist to pull him even closer. His arousal was evident through his tight-fitting jeans.

I broke off the kiss long enough to inhale some much-needed oxygen and whisper, "Bedroom, this way."

He stepped back and allowed me to lead the way, but didn't take his hands off me, which led to some stumbling and more kissing as we slowly traversed my small apartment. We made it as far as the couch in the living room before I gave up trying to make it any farther for now.

I put my hands on Brandon's broad shoulders and steered him into a sitting position. Kneeling over him, with my legs straddling his hips on the couch, gave me the upper hand and gave him a great view of my breasts. I leaned forward, kissing and licking my way up his neck on a leisurely path back to his lips as he reached under my shirt, the fingers of one hand trailing up and down my spine leaving tingles in their wake.

His other hand found my nipple, already taught with arousal, through the thin lace of my bra. His hand skated over my sensitive flesh lightly, then more deliberately until he finally pinched the small bud between his thumb and forefinger.

I groaned and ground myself against his hardness that was pressed against my center though still constrained by his jeans. I decided it was time to do something about that. Breaking off our kiss, I slid my way down his body until I was on the floor between his knees. Brandon seemed to get the hint and hurriedly unbuttoned his pants, lifting his hips to slide them down.

I stopped his hands as he reached for his boxers and he grinned in surprised delight before relaxing back into the soft couch cushions. I eased his boxers down his muscular thighs—god bless kickboxing! Finally, after a moment that felt like hours his erection sprang forth from its cotton plaid confines. I took his shaft in my hand and eased my mouth over the head. His moan of delight sent tingles down to my toes, and shocks of pleasure to my clit. Sitting back and enjoying himself apparently got old fast and he was soon reaching down my back and tugging my shirt off.

I reluctantly released him with a soft pop, and licked my lips as he pulled the fabric over my head. I took advantage of the momentary reprieve to stand and pull him with me so we could make our way to the bedroom. More stumbling and passion filled kisses ensued as we made our way through the room.

I kicked my bedroom door open as Brandon reached between us, frantically undoing my pants. I paused to shove them down my legs and Brandon ran his hands down my curves to the top of my black lace panties. He teased me, running his fingers under the hem along my waist just a little bit too high, and he knew it!

The teasing didn't last long, however as he sank to a crouch and slowly pulled the thin fabric down my legs to the ground. He stood, trailing his hands all the way back up my body, leaving goosebumps in their wake and I half-stepped, half-stumbled forward out of my panties and into his waiting arms.

I grabbed the hem of his shirt, the only thing he had left on, yanking it quickly up over his head, and tossed it behind me. He lifted me into the air, a firm grip on my behind with his strong hands, and I could feel his erection, long and solid, pressed hard against me. I steadied myself by gripping his shoulders hard and pressing my lips to his.

Mouths open and tongues dancing together, he stepped back until we tumbled onto my bed, a tangle of sweaty limbs panting with excitement. I rolled off of him and shimmied my way up the bed, reaching for the drawer in my nightstand. I pulled it open and watched Brandon's eyes fall on the condoms. He nodded slightly but didn't reach for one.

"Not just yet darlin'," he said with a smirk. Then he placed his hands on the inside of my thighs and eased them apart. Settling himself between my legs, he began kissing his way up from one ankle. He left soft, wet kisses all the way up the inside of one leg, across my center, deliberately avoiding the most crucial spot, and back down the inside of the other leg.

By the time he reached my other ankle I was a trembling, sopping mess. Desperate for contact, my hips lifted up off the bed and I could hear Brandon chuckling softly to himself. Without warning, he suddenly pressed his whole tongue to my wet core, and I moaned so loud I was glad for the firewalls separating my apartment from the neighbours.

He continued, running his tongue up and down, never in the same spot for more than a second, all the while deftly avoiding my throbbing clit.

"Please…" I begged, unable to wait another second.

As if that was what he was waiting for, he went straight to

work, flicking his tongue in the exact right spot and the orgasm I had been desperately craving immediately wracking my body. I was glad he still held my thighs, as my legs shook and I pressed a pillow over my mouth to muffle my pleasure induced scream. Brandon sat back on his heels and mirrored my earlier actions, licking his lips as he reached into the nightstand drawer.

He leaned over me and pressed his lips to mine. I could taste myself on his tongue and the memory of what had just transpired made me shiver with pleasurable anticipation.

"Ready?" he asked, lining himself up with my center.

"Oh yes," I moaned, grabbing the back of his neck and pulling his mouth back to mine. He thrust into me with one hard push, and my back arched up off the bed once more, meeting his thrust with my hips. We quickly fell into a rhythm, matching each other's thrusts and speed naturally, easily, as if we were made to do this together. My hands roamed all over his torso, feeling every muscled inch under my fingertips, committing it all to memory. He used one arm to hold himself up, and the other pulled down the cup of my lace bra, the one article of clothing we had neglected to discard. As our coupling became more frantic, both of us close to the edge, he pinched my nipple between his fingers. I moaned in response and Brandon, encouraged by my response, continued his ministrations and soon I was tipping over the edge again.

My fingernails trailed down his back as I writhed beneath him, my cunt pulsing with orgasmic pleasure. He released my breast and gripped my hip hard, thrusting his cock as deep as he could once, twice more, and with a groan of release, he stopped moving and his forehead dropped onto my shoulder.

We lay together, panting in each others ears for a few moments until he rolled off of me. I took a much-needed deep breath and my body relaxed into the bed, limbs feeling like jelly covered in sweat. I felt the weight of the bed shift as Brandon got up, likely in search of a garbage can. He bounced back onto the bed beside me on his side, propped up on one elbow.

"So," he said, "feel like continuing your private lessons on a regular basis?"

I placed one hand on each side of his face with a tired and satiated grin and pulled his mouth to mine in response. I guess I owe Isabella a thank you card.

END

Six

Game Night

The dice rang hard against the table as Alex rolled them. "Pay the lady!" I yelled, holding out my hand for his cash with a wink. "Sorry darling." I smiled and added his money to my stash. "Don't pout, I'll make it up to you," I added, running my hand up his leg under the table.

The dice passed to the next player and he reached under the table, gripping my hand and tugging it upward to feel the hard rod under the pants. I glanced sideways at him, grinning even wider. I squeezed gently and then released him to reach for the dice.

I landed on a safe space and watched as the other players made their way around the board, paying out various large amounts. As the dice came back around, and my hand made its way back up his lap, we decided to call the game.

"Everyone count up! Even though we're all pretty sure Michelle has beat the pants off us once again." Eliza called.

She was my best friend of twenty years, and engineer of this little *meet cute*. She had invited Alex over to join our board game night knowing that I would be the only other single person there who might be interested. Our other bestie, Samantha, had come alone—her girlfriend was at work—and Eliza's husband had declined to join in favour of watching the hockey game.

That left just the four of us to our rousing game of monopoly. During which I thoroughly kicked everyone's ass. Alex and I got on like a house on fire, and I wasn't too naïve to know what the aim of the evening was. He wasn't either. As evidenced by his wandering hands and semi uncomfortable pants issues.

We cleaned up the game board and pieces and Alex was suspiciously unhelpful, but that was likely due to his fingers playing up my spine under my shirt. His other hand dipped beneath the waistband of my pants, ever so slightly. I giggled involuntarily, and Eliza glanced over from where she was packing all the board game pieces into the box.

The sly smile on her lips only made my giggles worse, and Alex pulled his hands away with a questioning glance. Eliza shook her head sharply at him, indicating—I assumed—that he had been heading in the right direction.

"Sam!" She said, "Wanna help me take the dishes to the kitchen?" Eliza gathered up the game with some dishes piled on top of it and leaned her head towards the doorway.

"Yep! I definitely do!" Samantha replied, with a nod. She scooped up the rest of the dishes and followed Eliza out of the room, throwing me a wink over her shoulder.

Alex and I were left alone in the living room. His hands all too recently underneath my clothes. He smiled sheepishly in my direction and I cast my eyes downward.

I'm not a one night stand type of girl. But he was super hot, funny and friendly. It made secret parts of me feel warm and tingly. I decided to bite the bullet and take the plunge—is that a mixed metaphor? I didn't care.

I reached across and slipped my hand up under his button-down shirt. My hand crept around his back and pulled him close. His lips crashed into mine and we kissed fiercely, his hands running all over me. He pulled me into his lap and I stumbled out of my chair.

I landed across him, our lips still clashing, teeth and tongues meeting each other in a passionate dance. My legs draped across his lap and he grabbed the back of my neck, holding my mouth to his.

The hand that wasn't running across his muscled back gripped the front of my shirt fiercely. I shifted my lower half until my legs straddled his, his hardness pressed against my center. After another minute—or hour, or week? I had lost track of any semblance of time—I pulled my mouth away, desperate for oxygen. We gasped together, breathing each other's air, sweat trickling down our temples.

"I… need…" I squeaked out each word in between breaths, "need to get home. I have to work tomorrow."

"Oh, of course." Alex relinquished his vice like grip on my hips, his face clearly disappointed.

"I'd like to see you again, maybe tomorrow night if you're free?" I decided to take a chance and ask him out, something I wouldn't normally do. But I trusted my friends judgement. If they had picked him for me, it must've been for a good reason.

His grin was all I needed to back up my choice, and as he ran his finger tips up my spine I shivered and leaned in for another bruising kiss. I pulled my hand out of his shirt and gripped the back of his neck, holding his lips to mine as he had done so recently to me. I broke off and ran my lips and tongue along his jawline, kissed and licking my way up to his earlobe.

Once there I whispered, "Give me your phone."

He chuckled and pressed an open-mouthed kiss against my neck before pulling back enough to hand me his phone. I entered my information in the contacts section and handed it back.

"Text me tomorrow?" I asked, batting my lashes in an over the top flirtatious gesture.

He laughed aloud as he took his phone back. "Definitely." He nodded and pulled me in for another kiss, giving me only the briefest taste before standing up. His hands on my hips steadied me and put some distance between us. "Do you think we should tell Eliza and Sam it's safe to come back in?" He asked with a wry grin.

"Or we could make them think we're getting dirty in the dining room?" I countered.

He laughed and wrapped a muscled arm around my waist. "Don't think I didn't consider it," he said as he pressed his lips against my pulse point.

"Better not tempt us any further," I replied. "Eliza, Sam, you can stop listening from the kitchen now!"

***

Work the next day was an unbearable waiting game.

Alex had been sending me flirty text messages all afternoon, ever since we had confirmed our plans for the evening. He was taking me out to dinner, at a restaurant of his choosing. Which was good, as I was notoriously terrible at deciding what to eat.

I tried to get some work done, but ended up spending a more than appropriate amount of time staring blankly at my computer screen while sexy fantasies danced behind my eyes.

As the end of the day inched ever closer—the clock seemed to be deliberately taking forever to click over each minute—Sam's head poked around the corner of my office doorway.

"I know what you're doing tonight," she said in a singsong voice.

"Ha. Ha," I replied. "Would you please come in and close the door before we discuss my potential sex life?"

"Aha! I knew it!" Sam pumped her fist at her hip to underscore her excitement. She slipped around the doorframe and clicked the door shut behind her.

"Do you want a medal?" I asked with a raised eyebrow. "I was in the man's lap just last night. Are we surprised?"

"Of course not," Sam replied with a ridiculous grin, "I'm just glad to be the first to get verbal confirmation."

"Oh yeah?" I asked, skeptical. "And what is the bet on my sex life going to win you tonight?"

"A week of no dishes!" She said, while doing a happy dance around my small office. "So, spill what's the plan tonight? You are going out, obviously."

"We are," I said with a nod, "and in the interest of sparing you a week of dish duty, I fully intend to let that man ravish me after dinner. At his place or mine, I haven't decided yet." I smiled, mostly to myself, remembering the text messages I'd been receiving throughout the day.

"Omigod don't let him go to your place! Unless you're planning to have a hazmat team go through first." Sam's face was equal parts horrified and amused.

"Oh, fuck you Sam, not all of us are allergic to laundry," I said as we both doubled over laughing.

"Well, some people value cleanliness, 'Shell, excuse me for trying to assist your sex life," Sam said scathingly with a grin.

"Pretty sure if we get back to my place tonight, he's not going to be looking around my apartment. If he is, then he is the wrong choice, and I will blame you and Eliza," I replied as a smirk crossed my lips.

"Yes, well." Sam opened the door with delicate fingers, so as not to draw attention. "One day I'll teach you what a laundry basket is for." She laughed so hard her head rocked back, then she glanced over her shoulder. "Text me with details later?"

"Naturally," I replied, smiling though my eyebrows were still drawn together, giving a mock frown in response to her jab about my laundry habits. She smirked at me and closed the door behind her, leaving me at my desk with mixed feelings about fantasies and my messy apartment.

"No, no, no." I shook my head at my own reflection. Hands planted on my hips, I scowled at the mirror.

I had on my sexiest bra and panty set, which, if we're being honest, is my only matching bra and panty set. Several outfit choices lay discarded around me and on the bed. *Why is trying to pick a decent date outfit so difficult? I can't be the only woman this happens to,* I thought. I grabbed my phone off the nightstand to check the time and promptly began to hyperventilate.

Only thirty minutes to get dressed, finish my make up and then pretend to not be anxiously awaiting his text when he got here to pick me up. I decided to do my makeup first and then match the outfit to it afterwards.

While attempting to concentrate on my eyelids in the bathroom mirror, my mind drifted back to some of the texts we had sent each other earlier that day.

Alex
Hey sexy, how's work going?

Michelle

Good. Excited about tonight, you?

Alex
More than excited

Michelle
Ooo that's encouraging

Alex
I hope my boss doesn't check in today though. I'm not getting much work done.

Michelle
Why not?

Alex
Too distracted, thinking about last night.
Your lips are distracting.

Michelle
Just my lips? I've been thinking about your lips all day, and your hands, and other things...

Alex
What other things? Care to share, cuz I've been thinking *other things* about you too.

Michelle
Ooo I think you should share first.

Alex
Well...I've been thinking about how much more of your skin I'd like to feel.
Running my hands under the back of your shirt was just a teaser, I hope?

Michelle
Oh? You have high expectations my friend!
Hehe, but not much higher that mine

Alex

That's good to know, but you are avoiding my question.

Michelle

I did? Oops! I guess I should answer you.

Alex

Yes, you should. Hehe

Michelle

Well then, I see I have no choice. Orrrr, I could make you wait until later. That sounds like more fun lol

Alex

Tease! Lol I'll have to let you have your fun. I'd better get back to work.

I'm looking forward to tonight though.

Michelle

Me too! See you :P

Reminiscing about our flirty text conversation provided a welcome distraction. I sped through the last of my make up and was finally able to settle on a sexy but not over the top outfit of fitted slacks and a silk top trimmed with purple lace. I slipped my feet into some kitten heels—comfort over style. I had a deep admiration for women who could wear 4-inch-high heels, but I would never be one of them.

I checked the time on my phone—five minutes to spare! Giving myself an internal high five, I slipped my phone into my back pocket and double checked the contents of my purse. Wallet, breath mints, condoms, check. Receipts and random garbage, also check, but ain't nobody got time to deal with that.

My phone buzzed in my pocket, letting me know that Alex was waiting downstairs. I swallowed my nerves and headed out the door, excitement tingling up and down my spine.

The restaurant Alex brought me to was pub style on the corner of two busy streets, its patio spilling out around the corner right up to the sidewalk on both streets. Surrounded by wrought iron fencing, it was just busy enough to make our conversation private among the din but not impossible to carry on.

We were halfway through our food—the poutine at this place was amazing—when I decided to see if last night's intense physical attraction was a fluke or not. I started by subtly running my foot up the inside of his calf under the table. He blinked at me and grinned, his fork stopped in midair halfway to his mouth. With his free hand, Alex reached across the table and took mine resting on the table.

"You were saying?" I asked, my foot continuing its languid path up and down his leg.

"Something terribly unimportant and boring I'm sure," he replied. "I'd much rather focus on what you're doing with your foot under the table."

"Oh?" I asked, and abruptly pulled away, causing his face to fall into an exaggerated pout.

"Yes," he responded, and the next thing I felt was his foot now making its way slowly up and down my own calf. I tried to remain unaffected, twirling melted cheese around my fork and spearing another French fry.

"I believe you were telling me how you met Eliza?" I asked, and delicately plucked the fry off my fork with my teeth.

"Right, of course," he said, and slid his foot slowly down the length of my leg and back towards his side of the table. He didn't release my hand, however. His thumb drew lazy circles on the side of my own. "I met Eliza through work, she was doing some consulting in my office building. We landed a big contract six months ago and I guess it was enough to fund a remodel of the lobby. The interior decorating company Eliza works for, I can never remember what it's called-"

"Renew You Interior Designs," I supplied.

"That's it!" he said, nodding at me in thanks. "Anyways, they were hired for the job."

"And how did the remodel go? Or is it not finished yet?" I asked, footsie under the table forgotten as we were once again absorbed in conversation.

"It's done now, and it wasn't bad actually. I mean, no one wants to walk through a construction zone to get to their office every day, but the new lobby is awesome and the powers that be sprung for a new espresso machine for the staff lunch room when they were working out the expenses. Yay lattes!" A genuine smile broke across his features, not the coy or suggestive ones I had been getting so far. An appreciation for good coffee was also a plus for me.

"There's nothing like a good latte to start the day. Way better than standard office coffee fare," I said in response to his enthusiasm.

"Right?" His eyes lit up and we spent the next several minutes discussing our mutual love of fine espresso. We shared our favourite local café locations and latte flavours until our plates were empty and the ice at the bottom of our glasses had melted.

When the waitress walked by, Alex politely excused himself, asking for her attention and requested the bill.

Tingles trilled up my spine in anticipation as we waited for the bill to arrive. I tried to distract myself by swirling the dregs in the bottom of my glass. His foot resumed its lazy travel up my leg, pretty thoroughly cutting through my pitiful attempt at distraction from my already wet panties.

***

Paying the bill and exiting the restaurant passed in a hormone induced haze of horniness. I tried to pay my half of the bill but he deftly distracted me by running his fingers up the back of my arm with a feather like touch. The hairs on the back of my neck stood on end and goosebumps made me shiver.

Despite my intense distraction I managed to use the Uber app on my phone to get us a car while he was settling the bill. We didn't have to wait long on the sidewalk for the driver to pull up, this was probably best for any bystanders who didn't want to watch us try and fail to hide the fact that we were slipping our hands inside each other's clothes.

We managed to contain ourselves for the sake of the Uber driver, in an attempt to be at least remotely polite. But our propriety ended as soon as we were inside the downstairs door of my apartment building.

Alex pressed my back hard against the wall of the stairwell, both of his hands running roughly up my back under the shirt as his mouth crashed into mine. We started to make our way up the staircase—thankfully we only had one floor to go. We stumbled sideways, neither of us willing to relinquish the other's lips or tongue.

I frantically unbuttoned his shirt, stopping short of ripping it off when we separated to gasp for air. We stopped moving long enough to catch our breath and I managed to force out the word *Keys* while brandishing my bag with the hand that was not currently clutching his open shirt like a life raft.

"Right." He nodded and pressed his mouth to mine again, with an urgency that straddled the border between desperation and need.

I returned his fervour with my own for a few more moments

until my grip on my purse slacked the point that I dropped it on the floor, its contents jangling us out of our stupor.

"Keys," Alex said as he pulled his delicious lips away and took a full step back across the landing. His eyes were dark with lust and burned into me, and I had to tear my own gaze away to retrieve my purse and unlock the door. I jammed the key in the lock while Alex stepped up behind me and grabbed my ass, giving it a tight squeeze. I gasped and shoved the door open, stumbling through and dropping my purse on the table inside the door.

Alex followed me, and I kicked the door shut before pushing his shoulders back hard against it, sliding my hands into his already open shirt and down his arms to guide it to the floor. He gripped the back of my neck with one hand and pulled my mouth to his, his other hand slipping up the back of my shirt to deftly unhook my bra.

I giggled against his lips and leaned back far enough to draw my top up over my head then discard my bra before stepping back towards my bedroom. I curled my finger towards myself in a 'come hither' gesture that Alex laughed out loud at before grabbing my waist and spinning me around until I was once again against the wall, albeit closer to the bedroom this time.

"Really?" he asked between kisses. "You think you can make me come with one finger?"

I tried but couldn't contain the laughter bubbling up inside of me, "That is the worst joke I have ever heard!"

"Oh!" He gasped and pressed a hand mockingly to his chest. "You wound me madam!"

"Shut up and fuck me," I replied, and hooked my fingers into the belt loops of his jeans, pulling him with me as I walked backwards into my room.

"I live to serve," he said and pressed his lips against mine again.

We reached my room and quickly divested each other of our remaining clothes. I sat on the bed and pulled his boxers down his legs, already naked myself and eager to remove the last remaining obstacle.

His erection stood before me, impressive but not intimidating. I ran the flat of my tongue up his cock from base to tip, eliciting a low groan as he tipped his head back and fisted his hand in my hair. I grinned before taking him into my mouth and alternating between hard suction and long, languid licks. Alex's moans changed to breathy gasps and his hand slipped out of my hair to lean on my shoulder. With his other hand he reached down and fondled my breast, rolling my nipple lightly between his thumb and forefinger. He pinched, not too hard, but enough to make me moan with his cock down my throat and he dug his fingers into my shoulder in response.

"Okay," he said, pulling out of my mouth, "I would really like to not end the night right here."

I looked up at him and deliberately batted my eyelashes in a ridiculous manner. He grinned and put both hands firmly on my shoulders, pressing me back into the bed.I used my heel for leverage to center us and he lined himself up with my core.

"Hold up," Alex said, using one arm to balance and the other to grope for my nightstand drawer. "I hope there are condoms in here."

"There are," I replied and leaned up on my elbows to help.

"I got it," he said just before he tore open the condom packet with his teeth and rolled it over himself. He took a moment to line up again and looked me in the eyes. "Ready?"

"Oh, yes," I breathed, "now please!"

"I live to serve," he whispered in my ear as he thrust into me in one fluid motion.

My back arched and I cried out at the intrusion, pleasure coursing through me. I gripped his hips hard and lifted my own to meet him thrust for thrust. I left one hand on his hip and ran the other up his side to grasp his shoulder, my nails digging in with every press of his dick to my g spot.

Alex braced his body over mine with one hand, his rhythm never faltering, as he fisted his other hand in my hair. He pulled, hard enough to yank my head to the side, and I hissed at the pleasure and pain mingling and pushing me closer to the edge. My hand on his hip slipped around to his back side, pulling him into me deeper and deeper with every thrust. His hand in my hair slacked and he pressed it flat against the mattress, giving himself more leverage.

"Ugh, oh god!" He cried as he came.

I met him thrust for thrust until he was done and rolled to the side with him when he pulled out. We lay together panting for several minutes.

Finally Alex said, "I don't want to be presumptuous, but I don't think I can use my legs." He flashed me that fantastic grin that had drawn me in during board game night.

"You're welcome to sleep here," I said with a smile, "just pass me my phone."

reached over the edge of the bed to where my pants had been dropped to the floor and fished out my phone. I grabbed it and quickly opened my messages app.

"I just have to send off a quick message to Sam," I said.

"You're kidding!?" Alex raised an eyebrow, but laughed at the same time.

"Oh! It's not what you think!" I replied and quickly typed out the message, tilting my phone so he could see what I was

typing.
Michelle
He never even noticed my laundry pile!

70

END

Seven

Moving Day

*L*oud knocking on the door drew my attention away from the last of the boxes I was taping up. Moving is such a pain—at least the packing and cleaning parts. Unpacking and organizing isn't so bad, but I still had to get all my stuff over to my new place first. The knocking indicated the arrival of my hired help. There was no way I was moving all these boxes by myself.

I stood and wiped my hands on the thighs of my tight skinny jeans. Not ideal for moving in, but the rest of my clothes were packed. I straightened my plain black tank top and answered the door.

On the other side stood two of the handsomest men I had seen in a long while. One had short cropped blonde hair and the other was a shaggy brunette.

"Hi, guys! I'm Kara," I said, holding my hand out.

"Pleasure to meet you ma'am, I'm Jean," said the blonde, "and this here is Lorne." He tipped his head towards his quiet partner.

"Oh god, don't call me ma'am!" I replied with mock disgust. "Just Kara is fine."

Both men grinned and I stepped back to let them in the door.

"Alright Kara," said Jean, "where do you want us to start?"

"Well I'm just finishing up with the boxes in here, you guys can start bringing the stuff out of my bedroom. The bed is disassembled already and everything in there is packed up," I said, indicating down the hallway to my bedroom.

Both men headed that way with a brief nod in my direction and I took advantage of a quick second to check them out from behind. Their faded jeans and tight, thin t-shirts showed off the muscles they both had from spending all day moving boxes and furniture. I shook my head against the distraction and went back to taping up boxes.

Within minutes they shifted my mattress and box spring down the hallway—a king sized I had splurged on. They reached the door and stopped while Lorne went out to back the truck up to the front steps.

I was glad for the hundredth time that my apartment was on the ground floor. And my new place was an actual honest to goodness house! No trekking boxes up to a fourth floor walk up. I still had nightmare flashbacks on moving in and out of my first apartment. Long before I could afford movers or a truck. My friends and I did the whole thing alone with one pick up truck. It had taken all day.

With a loud bang, Lorne lined up the truck ramp to the top step and the two men began moving my things out at a rapid pace. I picked up my own in order to finish taping up and packing the last-minute boxes. As I labeled the last one—living room misc, very organized I know—I figured I might as well give them a hand hauling boxes. I started carrying boxes to the truck bed only to have Jean step in front of me, a lopsided grin on his face.

"Now now ma'am, what do you think you're doing? Moving boxes is our job," he said.

"Oi! What did I say about calling me ma'am?" I replied, though I could tell he was teasing me. "And I know it's your job but I'm not about to sit around and do nothing. Just tell me if I'm putting anything in the wrong spot."

"Are you sure? You are paying us you know; it would be completely acceptable for you to 'sit around and do nothing,'" he countered.

"Yes, I'm sure," I said, shifting the weight of the box in my arms. "Kindly get out of my way now?" I smiled sweetly, tilting my head to the side.

"Alright, alright." Jean held his hands up in mock surrender. "Do what you want." He laughed and headed to the kitchen to continue loading boxes of dishes onto the dolly.

I smirked to myself, pleased with my success, and made my way into the back of the truck. Lorne was there taking boxes that had been dropped off by the dolly and stacking them strategically in the truck to maximize weight distribution.

"What are you doing in here?" he asked, his voice soft and tone not nearly as forceful as his partner's.

"Oh just pitching in," I said, daring him to tell me not to. Something told me he wouldn't be as quick to tell me what I shouldn't be doing.

"Oh," he replied, confirming my suspicions.

"Where do you want me to put this one?" I asked, lifting the box in my arms slightly.

"You can just leave it at the end of the truck bed there, I'll sort them as I go. And, um, thanks." He smiled for the first time since they had arrived, a shy smile that lit up his face, making his eyes sparkle. I was drawn in for a moment and caught myself starting, entranced by the change in his expression. I came back to myself, dropping the box lightly where he had indicated and went back inside.

We powered through the rest of the stuff and before I knew it, we were heaving the last boxes onto the truck.

"Awesome!" I exclaimed, surprised we were done so quickly. Although this *was* my first time hiring real live movers and not just roping my friends in with promises of beer and pizza. I straightened up after depositing the last box and swiped my hand across my sweaty forehead. My shirt stuck tight to my torso and when I turned around, and I caught both men openly staring at me, admiration clear on their faces.

I smirked when they blushed, Lorne more obviously than Jean and he turned his eyes away whereas the latter man made direct eye contact and answered my smirk with one of his own. I was sure he must have noticed me gawking at the two of them myself a few times over the last couple of hours.

"We're gonna head over to the new address and start unloading while you finish cleaning and locking up here, sound good *Kara?*" His deliberate emphasis on calling me by my name instead of ma'am made me laugh.

"Yeah sure," I said, tossing the keys to my new house at them.

Jean fumbled the catch but his partner, while quiet and reserved, apparently had lightning fast reflexes and snatched them out of the air.

"Nice catch," I said with a low whistle. "I'll see you guys soon then yeah? I shouldn't be long."

"See you soon, *Kara,*" Jean replied, and Lorne elbowed him in the side as they headed out to the truck.

I swept and mopped as quickly as I could, my mind replaying all the lingering looks and flirtatious commentary that had passed between us throughout the morning. Even Lorne had started to open up a little, although he looked scandalized at the some of the comments that came out of his partners mouth. My memories gradually faded into fantasies as I thought about the fun the three of us could have together. I wondered if they would be interested—in my experience most men were—and they seemed pretty close, close enough to share even.

Better get over to the new house then, I thought with a grin. One last check to make sure nothing was being left behind and I grabbed my things, left the key on the counter for the landlord and locked the door of my apartment for the last time.

***

I pulled up on the street in front of my new house. The driveway was blocked by the moving truck, the guys already hard at work unloading all my boxes. I jumped out of the car and jogged up the path to help out. The faster we got the stuff unloaded the faster we could get the bed set up, and I could enact my plan.

I was pleasantly surprised to see the truck half empty already, and the last of the unloading went quickly and easily. There was way more room in my new place than in the old one, so finding somewhere to put everything wasn't a problem. Soon I was directing the two men as they carried my box spring and mattress down the narrow hall to my new room. I had already taken the time to put the frame together so all they had to do was drop the other pieces on top.

"Just a couple more things to unload and we'll be out of your hair," Lorne said as they eased the mattress down onto the box spring.

"Oh not too quickly I hope," I replied with a wink.

Jean caught my action and threw me a curious look. I raised my eyebrows in response and his expression changed to one of surprise, then glee.

"Let's go get that stuff bud," he said quickly, grabbing his dark haired friend by the arm and damn near yanking him out of the room. I could hear their whispers as they retreated down the hall. Message received then, excellent.

I located the bag of bedroom stuff that contained my bed clothes and set about adding sheets, a comforter and pillows to the newly assembled piece of furniture. I could hear the semi distant sound of the two men quickly unloading the rest of the truck, followed by the tell tale banging of the ramp being put back up, and lastly the click of the door being closed.

The distinct sounds of two people removing their boots echoed through the house, with nothing unpacked to muffle the sounds, they carried easily.

I situated myself in a sexy, come-hither position on the bed and waited. Jean came through the door first, a wide smile on his face as he drank me in with his eyes. Lorne lingered in the doorway, but his blonde friend wasn't as shy. He approached quickly and stood beside the bed, looking at me like I was water and he was a man dying of thirst. He held eye contact with me—not moving—waiting I assumed, for my go ahead.

I nodded and he quickly pressed his lips against mine. I moaned in grateful relief of the sexual tension that had been building for hours, winding my arms around his neck. He lifted his legs and knelt over me, the bed dipping from one side to the other as he situated himself. I broke off the kiss for a moment and glanced over to where Lorne still stood in the doorway, his mouth open but his arousal evident through his tight faded jeans. I removed one hand from around his friend's neck and beckoned him.

"Don't be shy," I said with a wink.

The darker haired man stumbled towards us, unsure on his feet but certainly eager to join in. He climbed onto the bed and knelt behind me. I followed his movement with my eyes until he was settled on his knees then grabbed the back of his neck with my free hand and pressed my lips to his. His kiss was different from Jean's, softer and more exploratory where the former's had been rough and forceful. It was a nice contrast.

Speaking of the other party, he took advantage of my distraction to slip a hand beneath my shirt and palm my breast, tweaking the already hard nipple, eliciting a squeal of pleasure from my mouth.

I released Lorne's mouth and turned to face the other man who's self satisfied smirk greeted me as he continued his ministrations beneath my shirt. I took a second to remove the interfering fabric, allowing much easier access to my smooth skin and pert tits.

Behind me, large, calloused hands slid up and down my now naked back, leaving a trail of heated skin in their wake. I arched into the hands—a pair now—that worked their magic on taut nipples. Shy but emboldening fingers crept around from my back to my slender waist, dipping closer and closer to hem of my pants. My head dropped back against the shy man's shoulder as he deftly undid my jeans. He popped the button and slowly slid the zipper down. I shivered with pleasure and anticipation but forced myself to lean up a moment and set about divesting them both their shirts.

I now had an open display of beautiful maleness to drink

in, as we resituated ourselves on the bed. I lost my jeans somewhere in the shuffle and found myself happily pressed between two hard bodies. My heart pounded in my chest, hot blood coursing through my veins, inflaming my skin. The excitement was palpable in the air between us. Four hands roamed over the planes of my body, over my hips and ass. Pinching and squeezing in all the right places.

I kissed my way down Jean's neck until he pulled my face to his and crashed our lips together in a bruising kiss. I reached between us to stroke his length as I felt someone's fingers—I wasn't sure who's to be honest—slipping beneath the sheer fabric of my panties, stroking my already wet folds. I groaned against the hard mouth pressed to mine and tightened my grip on his cock. The fingers moved up and down, teasing my clit but not getting quite close enough, didn't react however. Which gave me a clue as to who they belonged to. I broke off the kiss with a gasp when those same fingers suddenly plunged inside me.

My back arched and Jean took advantage of my breasts being put on such obvious display, his rough hands making my nipples almost painfully hard. Every touch shot to my core, which Lorne so expertly played like an instrument that had been made just for him. All the stimulation brought me to the brink of orgasm before I had time to catch my breath.

"Let go," the dark-haired man whispered in my ear and just like that, I came undone. My hips pumped erratically against his hand and I could hear one or both of them moan in excitement at watching me cum.

My limbs went limp and I flopped onto my back with a contented sigh. Jean was on top of me in seconds, easing my sopping panties down my legs and discarding them off the side of the bed. He coaxed my knees apart and settled himself between them, his rock-hard length teasing my entrance. He sank into me and my eyes rolled back in my head at the sensation of fullness. I hadn't quite realized his size until now.

We found a rhythm quickly as he pounded my already sensitive flesh, every contact sending jolts of pleasure through my belly. It took me a moment to realize someone was missing, I turned my head and found Lorne kneeling beside my shoulders, watching us with his mouth slightly agape. He was stroking his considerably large cock almost absentmindedly, too entranced in the show we were putting on.

"Come here," I panted, and he looked at me questioningly, tearing his attention away from watching Jean piston in and out of me. I made my meaning plain by opening my mouth wide with raised eyebrows. I watched as his cock twitched with excitement once he realized what I meant, and he shuffled over to me.

He lined himself up with my mouth and pushed forward while I sucked him deep into my throat. He groaned in ecstasy and fisted his hand in my hair, holding me to him as he fucked my mouth. My eyes drifted closed as I focused on both cocks in me at once, relaxing my throat to take the one in my mouth as deep as I could while meeting the thrusts of the other with my hips.

It wasn't long before I was spiralling to the edge of oblivion again, overwhelmed and full from two very different angles. The hand holding my hair tightened suddenly, bordering on painful but I didn't mind, and hot cum hit the back of my throat. He stopped moving and gave me a moment to swallow before pulling out and collapsing beside us. He didn't lay there for long though, one hand snaked down between our bodies to find my aching clit and with the other he pinched a nipple lightly, rolling it between his fingers.

The extra stimulation was all I needed to crest that edge I'd been dangling over, my back arched, and I lost all ability to think straight, let alone keep up with Jean's increasingly frantic thrusts. My scream of pleasure dwindled off to a moan as I came down from the dizzying heights they had brought me to. Just in time for the man on top of me to lean down and capture my lips in another of his bruising kisses as he succumbed to the pleasure as well, moaning out loud against my lips.

We fell into a tangle of sweat covered limbs, all three of us panting with exhaustion, our skin flushed pink from the exertion. Seconds stretched into minutes as we caught our breaths and came back to ourselves.

Eventually I sat up, and took in the mess of clothing scattered on the floor and half off the bed, evidence of our frantic coupling, or is it tripling? I looked over my shoulder at the two men. Jean looked smug and Lorne had gone back to looking shy and awkward, despite the fact that he was still naked on my bed and I could still taste his cum in my mouth.

I giggled when a thought floated through my slightly dazed mind. "I'm starving, you guys wanna get a pizza?"

Jean grinned and wrapped his arm around my waist, pulling me back between them on the bed. "Maybe," he said, and ran his fingers slowly up my naked thigh to the dip at my waist and the down below my belly button, "in an hour or two."

I looked over at Lorne, whose shy smile told me everything I needed to know. I settled back on the bed between the two men again. I guess the pizza can wait a while.

END

About the Author

Lucy Luscious is the romance and erotica pen name for Nova Scotia author Emerald Baynton. When she's not writing she can be found baking, reading, homeschooling her kids and trying out pretty much every craft under the sun. Follow her blog full of book release updates, and a lot of pictures of food.

You can connect with me on:

- http://www.emeraldscreations.org
- http://www.twitter.com/emeraldb85
- https://www.instagram.com/emeraldb_author

Read a brand new series staring shy virgin Aliyah Shaw and dominant lawyer Elliot Thomas. New to Amazon November 2020, start the series for just 99 cents today!

Aliyah's Surrender: Discovering Desires Book 1

Aliyah Shaw is a 24 year old receptionist with dreams of becoming a teacher. She just went into the cafe to get a latte, she had no idea she would meet Elliot Thomas. The unbelievably sexy lawyer who was about to turn her world upside down. Elliot always gets what he wants and today he wants Aliyah.